# SUPER DC HEROES

# SUPERMAN

## SUPER-VILLAIN SHOWDOWN

WRITTEN BY
PAUL KUPPERBERG

ILLUSTRATED BY
ERIK DOESCHER, MIKE
DeCARLO, AND LEE
LOUGHRIDGE

SUPERMAN CREATED BY
JERRY SIEGEL AND
JOE SHUSTER

STONE ARCH BOOKS
MINNEAPOLIS    SAN DIEGO

Published by Stone Arch Books in 2010
151 Good Counsel Drive, P.O. Box 669
Mankato, Minnesota 56002
*www.stonearchbooks.com*

Library of Congress Cataloging-in-Publication Data

Kupperberg, Paul.
  Super-villain showdown / by Paul Kupperberg ; illustrated by Erik
Doescher.
     p. cm. -- (DC super heroes. Superman)
  ISBN 978-1-4342-1570-3 (lib. bdg.) -- ISBN 978-1-4342-1736-3 (pbk.)
 [1. Superheroes--Fiction.]  I. Doescher, Erik, ill. II. Title.
  PZ7.K87Sup 2010
  [Fic]--dc22
                                  2009010366

Summary: Intergalactic peacekeepers are chasing the evil Terra-Man
through space! When this super-villain seeks refuge on Earth, Superman
offers to join the peacekeepers' posse. Soon, the Man of Steel locates the
gun-slinging criminal in an Old West ghost town, and the two face off in
an old-fashioned showdown.

Art Director: Bob Lentz
Designer: Brann Garvey

Printed in the United States of America

# TABLE OF CONTENTS



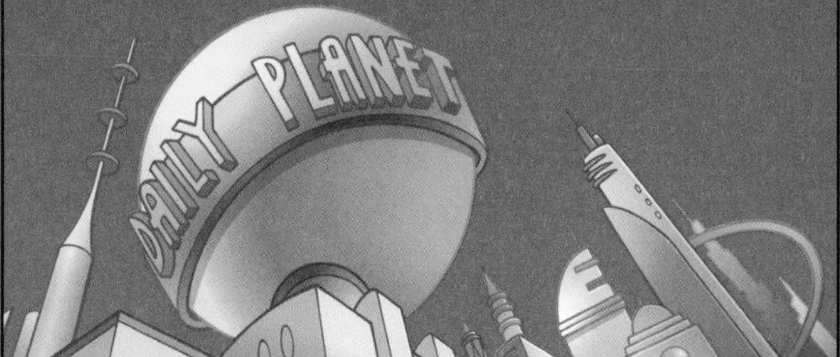
DAILY PLANET

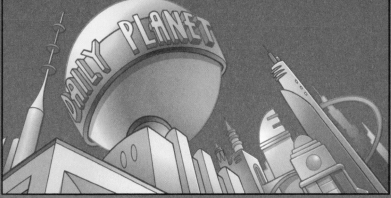

# CHAPTER 1

# A WALK IN THE HILLS

It wasn't often that Clark Kent had time to do something other than work. Clark had two jobs. Both jobs were full-time, and both were very demanding. Everyone knew he was a reporter for the Metropolis *Daily Planet* newspaper. Clark spent many long hours every day writing important stories about people who broke the law or cheated the public.

When he wasn't reporting, Clark had another job. He was Superman — the legendary Man of Steel.

Born on the planet Krypton, Superman gained superpowers and abilities from the yellow rays of Earth's sun. Superman's help was in constant demand all over the world and beyond. As both Clark Kent and Superman, the hero used his skills to keep the world safe.

Clark was spending his day off from the *Daily Planet* exploring the Old West. There were no Superman-sized threats that needed his attention. So, he had some time to relax.

One of the advantages of being Superman was super-speed. It took him only a few minutes to fly anywhere in the world. Clark had loved old Western shows when he was a boy. It made him curious to visit a town where those stories had taken place.

Clark walked through the hills of Arizona's Painted Desert. It was called that because of the amazing colors of its desert landscape. It was home to one of the greatest stories Clark had ever read.

In the 1890s, the outlaw Jess Manning and his eight-year-old son, Tobias, traveled together across the Wild West. Whenever Manning would rob a stagecoach, train, or bank, he left the boy hidden along his escape route in the care of his trusty stallion, Nova.

One day, Manning Big and Manning Little came to town. After a stagecoach robbery, the outlaws vanished. No one knows for sure where they went. But the outlaws were last seen in these very hills.

Clark was certain he could solve the mystery of the missing outlaws.

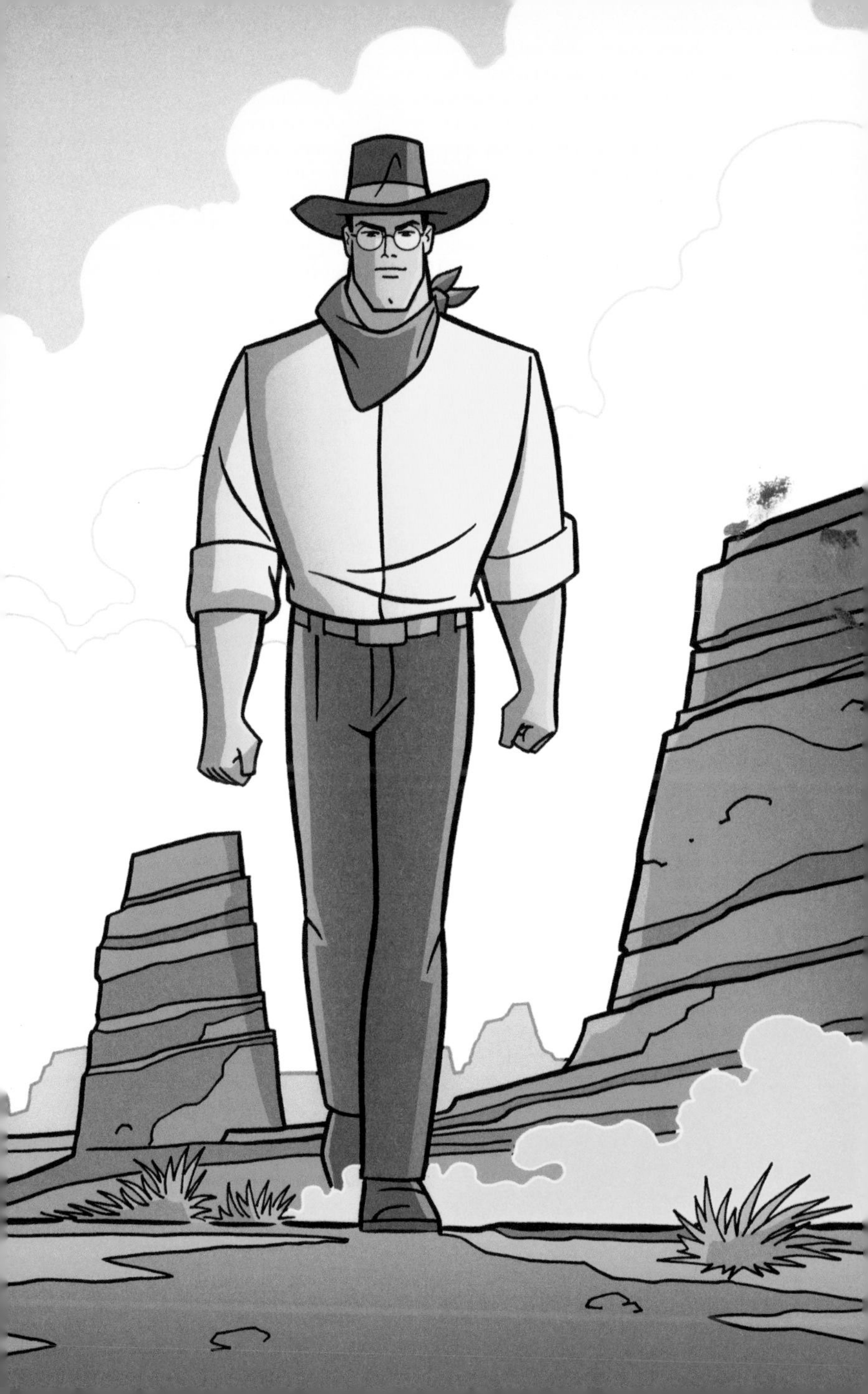

Clark followed the old trail through the mountains where the outlaws had disappeared 120 years ago. The trail cut through the harsh ground. It was surrounded by walls of granite, giant boulders, scruffy plants, and sun-baked rocks. There were even caves farther along the trail. Many people believed the Mannings had gotten lost in them as they tried to escape.

Many people had searched for signs of the lost Mannings ever since, but the duo's fate remained a mystery.

Clark smiled. "I'll have an edge in solving this mystery," he said to himself. "I'll be the first person to look for them who has X-ray vision!"

One of Superman's powers was the ability to see through solid objects.

Superman's eyes worked like an X-ray machine in a doctor's office. As he walked, he scanned the hills with his X-ray vision. He peered inside the caves beneath their rocky face.

While he was looking at the ground, Clark Kent suddenly heard a strange sound from above. **WHIR-WHIR-WHIR-WHIR!** He took off the glasses he wore as a disguise and looked up using his super-vision. It allowed him to magnify faraway sights with ease.

Five flying objects streaked like fiery meteors through the sky. Each object was actually a ship with someone riding it. Suddenly, Clark realized that the ships were headed right for him!

"So much for my day off," Clark said with a sigh.

The mild-mannered reporter removed his clothing faster than the eye could see. In a blur, Superman appeared in his blue and red uniform that was hidden underneath. "This looks like a job for Superman!" he said.

With a mighty leap, Superman shot up, up, and away and into the sky.

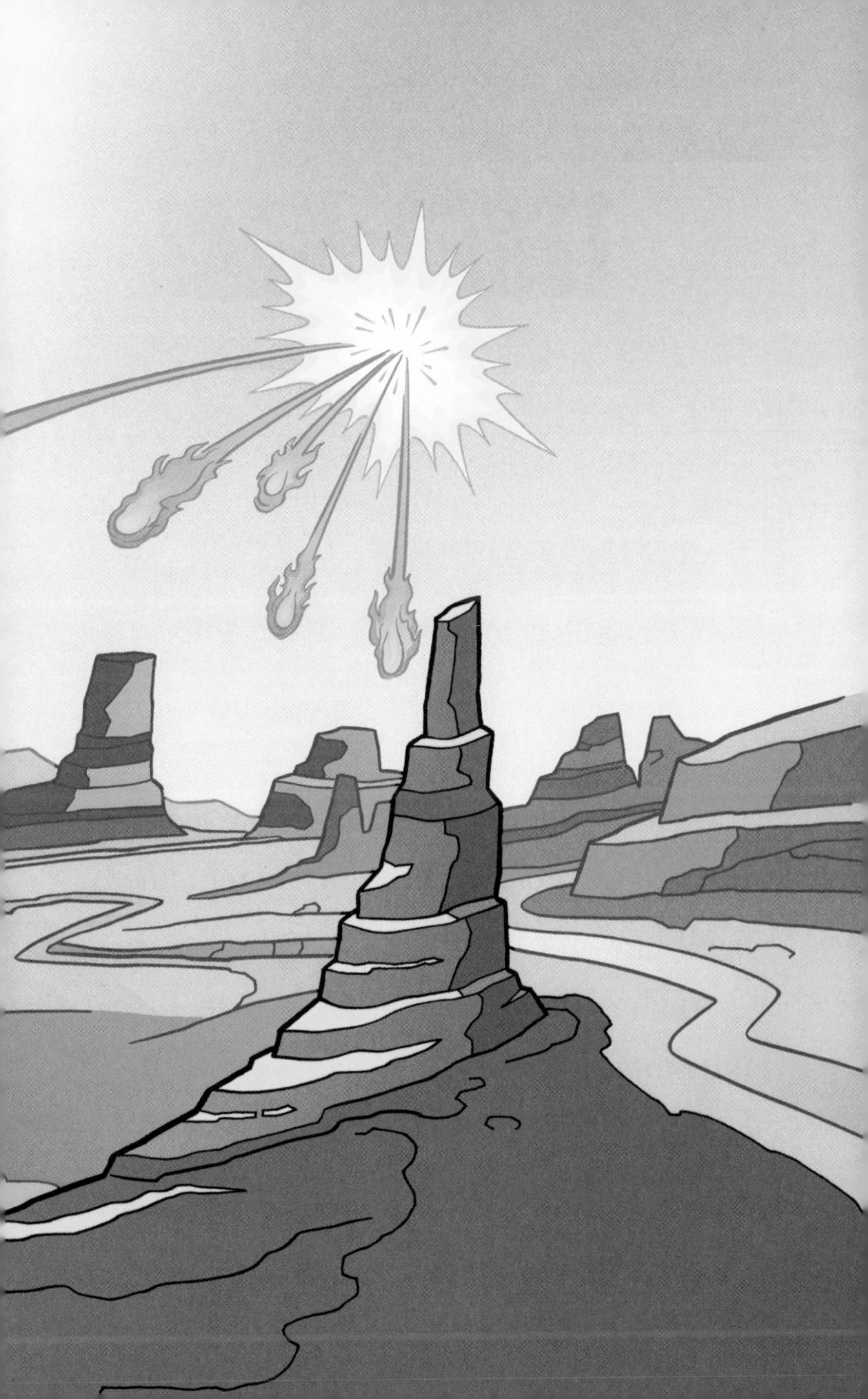

# CHAPTER 2

# TERRA-MAN!

**WHOOOOSH!** In a blue streak, Superman flew toward the flying ships.

"Stop!" he yelled. His super-loud voice rumbled like thunder through the sky. Superman would not attack before learning what the visitors wanted, but he remained cautious.

The five ships stopped when they neared the Man of Steel. The vehicles reminded Superman of motorcycles without wheels. Each airship carried a strange alien being.

The aliens were dressed in identical spacesuits. Each wore the same star-shaped symbol on its chest. Sashes around their bodies held energy blasters and other equipment, just like a policeman's belt. Each ship was surrounded by an invisible force field. The shields protected the riders from the intense cold of deep space.

"We come in peace, Superman!" said one of the aliens. "We are lawmen, just like you."

"You know who I am?" asked the Man of Steel.

"All of the universe knows who you are, Superman!" said the alien. "That is why we have come. I am Balther, leader of this team. It is an honor for us to meet the great Superman."

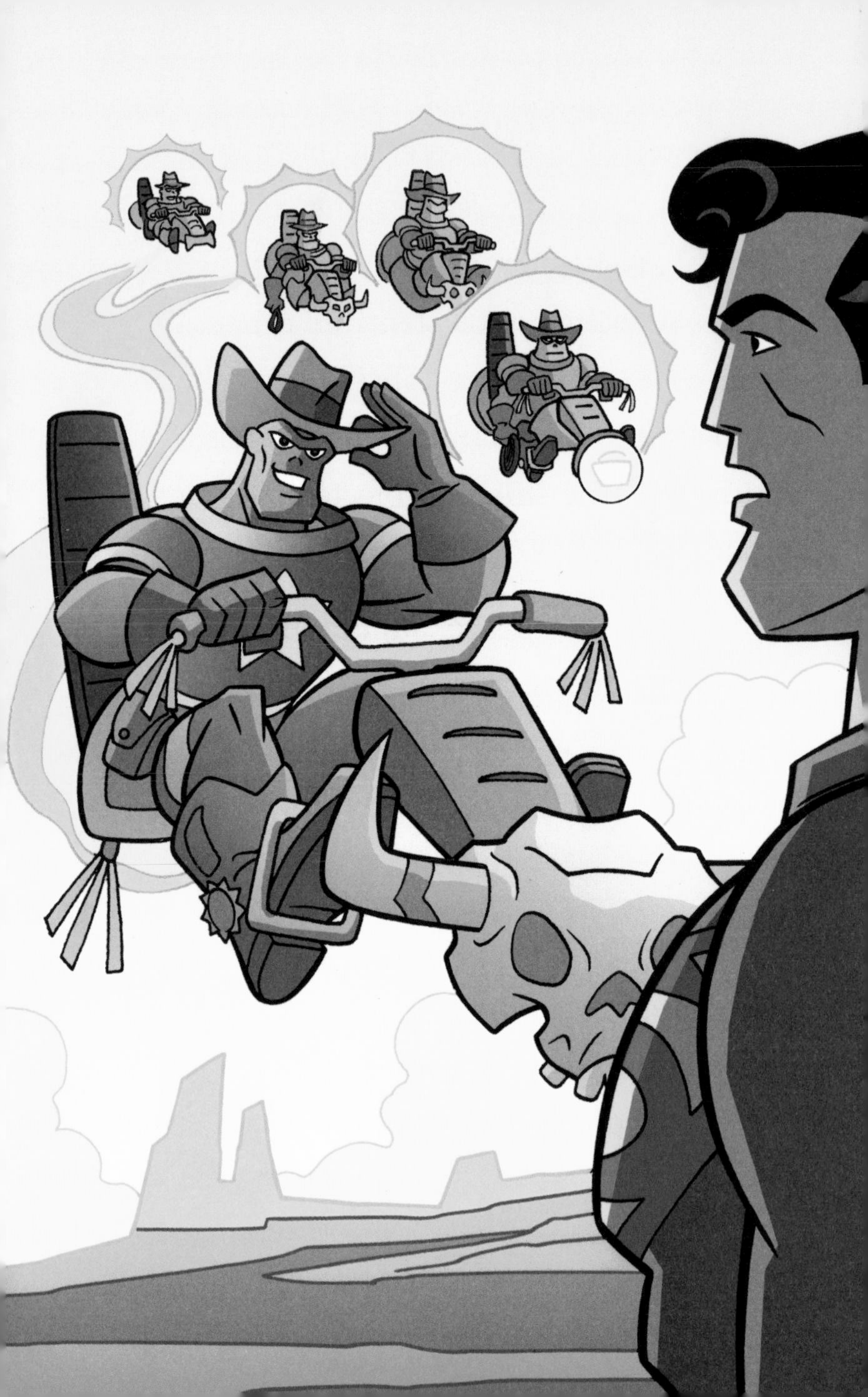

"Thank you," Superman said. "What brings you to Earth, Balther?"

"We are on the trail of the outlaw known as Terra-Man," said Balther. "He is very dangerous."

"I've never heard of Terra-Man," Superman said.

"He is an evil and dangerous man," said a blue-skinned alien. "I am Tyrox. I have seen the cruel things Terra-Man has done. He cannot be trusted."

A different alien with rocky skin and three arms and three legs moved forward.

"I am Charop," said the alien. "We have tracked Terra-Man here. We believe he is hiding in the Painted Desert. He was born here on Earth more than one hundred years ago."

"His father was an outlaw," Charop continued. "He died in a fight with an alien known as the Collector. The Collector's ship had landed in the hills below, for unknown reasons. That is where the earthling outlaw found him."

"The human was frightened by what he saw. So he drew his weapon," Tyrox added. "But the Collector was faster, and he won their duel. The Collector took the human's child into space. He raised him as his own son, and trained him to become the greatest outlaw who ever lived."

"He does sound dangerous," said Superman. "I think you should let me take care of this Terra-Man by myself."

"Of course, Superman," said a tall, purple man called Gyyhwn.

"We are guests on your world, and we will do as you ask. But be careful," Gyyhwn warned. "The Collector made Terra-Man into something more than human. His powers and weapons are great."

"Where I can find him?" asked Superman.

"Terra-Man came from a place known as Cripple Creek, Arizona," Charop said.

Superman smiled. "That's not far from here," he said. "By the way, what was Terra-Man's original name?"

When Superman heard the name Balther spoke, his eyes went wide with surprise. "Great Krypton!" Superman gasped. "So that's what happened to the Mannings!"

# CHAPTER 3

# THE ROUND-UP

Cripple Creek was a deserted ghost town. The wooden buildings and stores along Main Street were falling apart. Some were missing roofs. Others had collapsed long ago. All of them were covered with dust. Sand blew through the empty windows and doors of every building.

Superman stood at one end of Main Street. Everything was silent except for the whisper of the wind that pushed along a few tumbleweeds. The scene reminded him of the old Westerns on television.

In the distance, the Man of Steel heard the familiar whinny of a horse. At the end of the street, Superman saw something. A dark figure emerged from the shadow of a building.

"Howdy, Superman," the figure said. He stepped into the sunlit street and turned toward the Man of Steel.

Superman was surprised. He had expected Terra-Man to look like an astronaut wearing a spacesuit. But the space outlaw was dressed like a cowboy from the future. He wore a wide-brimmed hat, a long cape, and boots just like a cowboy from the Old West. His outfit was made with a strong metal that covered his body. A shiny metal belt held two energy weapons in holsters. An energy whip was coiled at his side.

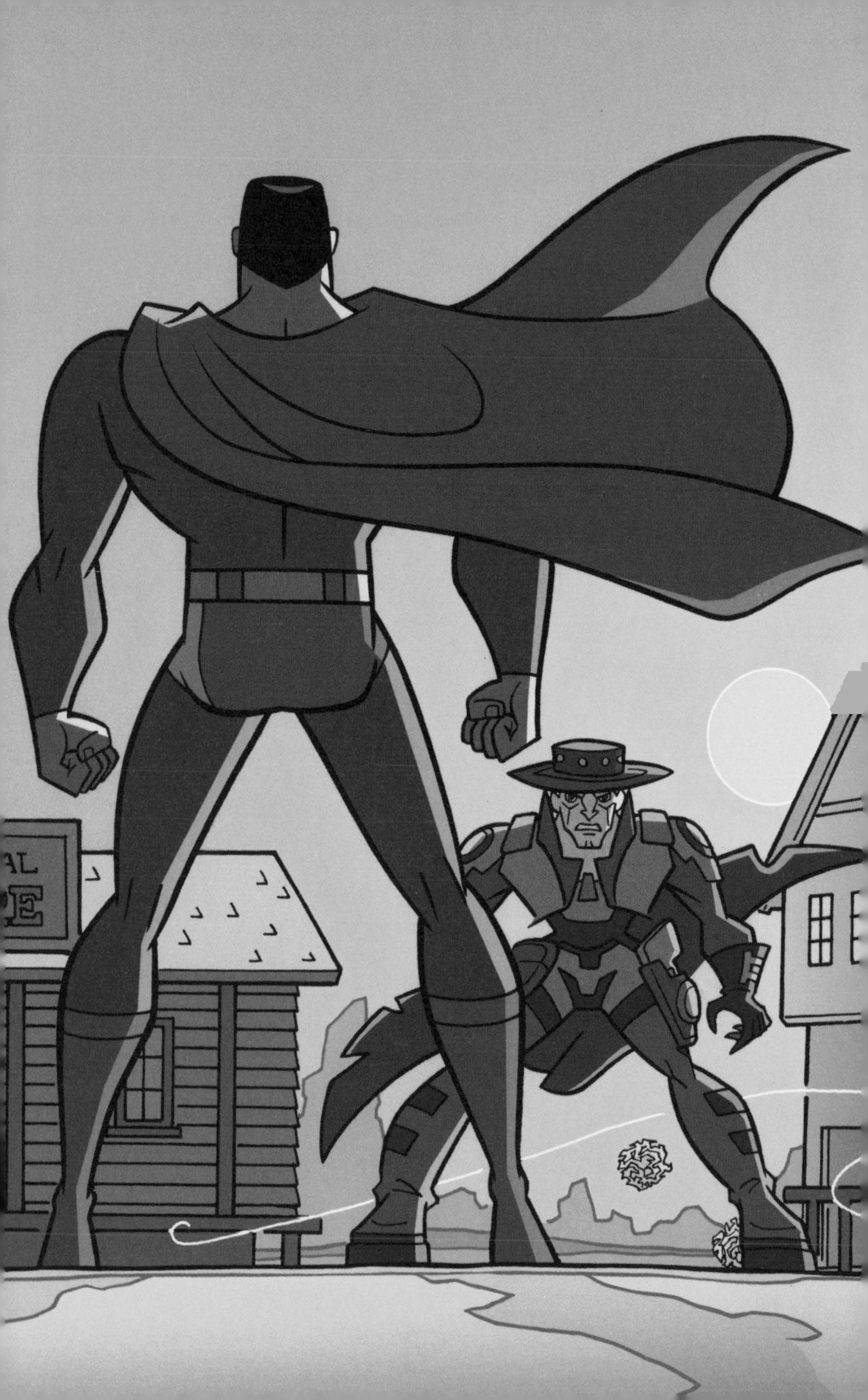

"Terra-Man, I'm here to place you under arrest," said Superman.

"I reckon you can try," said the outlaw, smiling. "But don't expect me to come peacefully."

Faster than the human eye could see, Superman flew at super-speed toward Terra-Man. The Man of Steel would have the outlaw in jail before he could even finish bragging.

Terra-Man vanished! Suddenly, he was at the other end of the street. The outlaw grinned at Superman.

*He's moving faster than I can see!* Superman thought to himself.

"I'm harder to catch than a greased pig, partner," the outlaw said, laughing.

"Best you give up trying to catch me and save your breath!" Terra-Man said.

Superman rocketed upward until he was just a distant dot in the sky. Terra-Man glanced up, but never lost his smile. He stuck his fingers between his lips and whistled long and loud.

Superman flew higher until he knew Terra-Man could no longer see him. Then, at super-speed, he dove back down toward Cripple Creek. He flew in big, fast circles. He hoped he would catch Terra-Man off-guard.

Just as Superman passed the highest rooftop in town, another flying object shot out of the sky.

It crashed into the Man of Steel.

The collision sent Superman tumbling out of control. He was moving so fast that when he had finally stopped, he was hundreds of miles away.

Superman shook his head. "What hit me?" he said. "How can he move so fast that even *I* can't see it coming?"

As Superman sped back to Cripple Creek, the answer to that question flew straight toward him.

"What is that?" Superman gasped.

It was a horse — a flying horse with wings! Seated on the stallion's saddle was Terra-Man. In one hand, he held the reins. In his other, he held an energy blaster.

"This here's Nova," Terra-Man said. "He's a mustang. He used to belong to my pa, the outlaw Jess Manning!"

"My alien step-pa upgraded old Nova," Terra-Man said. "Now Nova's invulnerable, just like you. And he can travel faster than any spaceship!"

Terra-Man gave Nova's reins a shake. Then the winged horse flew forward. Its front legs kicked at Superman. The Man of Steel dropped below its hooves and swooped under the animal.

Nova spun faster than Superman thought any living creature could move. This time, its hammering hooves found their mark. They struck the Man of Steel in his chest.

Superman went spinning through the air. Before he could stop himself, Terra-Man aimed at him with his energy blaster.

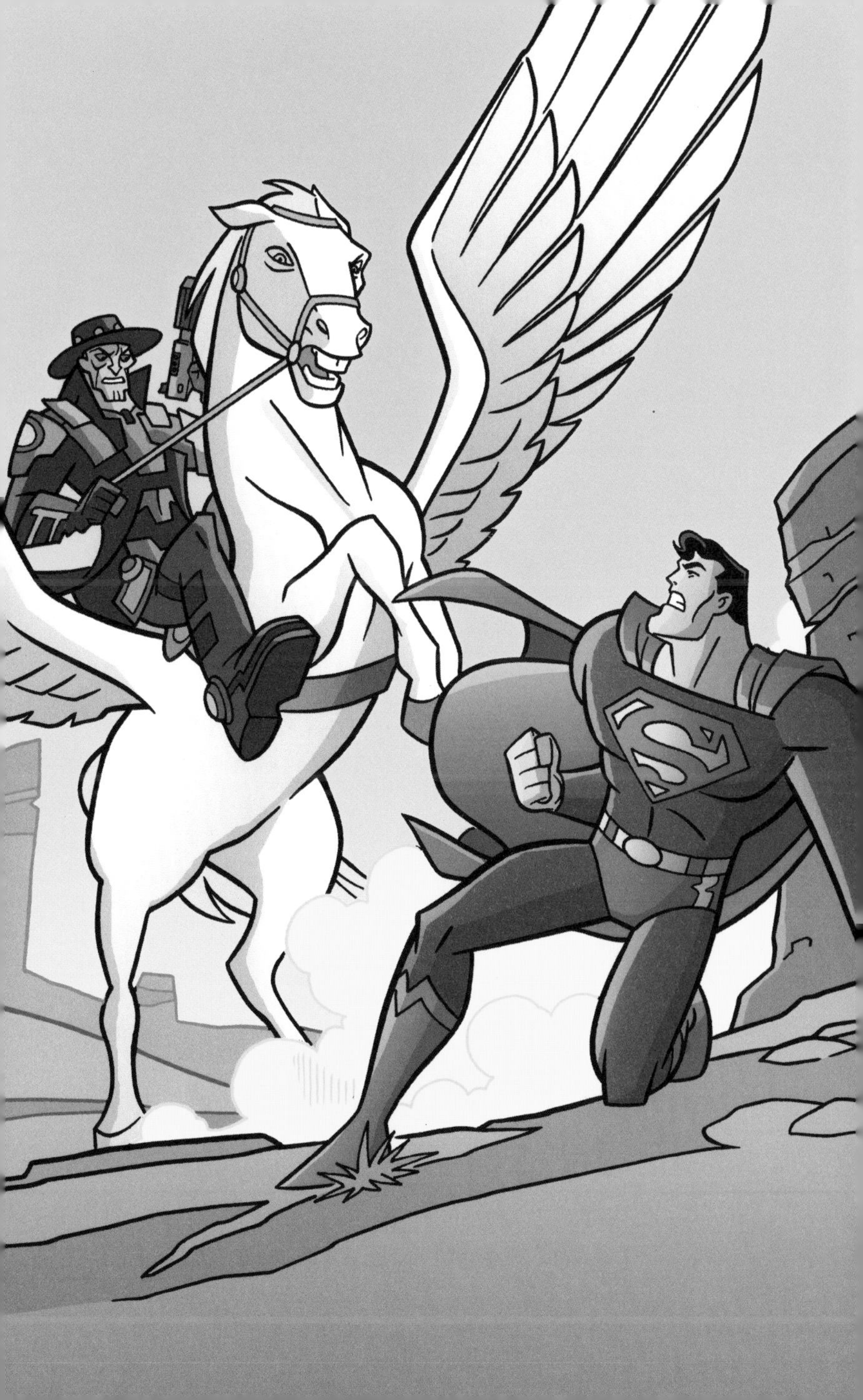

"Let's see if I can hit a moving target," said Terra-Man.

Superman chuckled at the thought of such a weapon being able to hurt him. Then he remembered Gyyhwn's warning: "His powers and his weapons are great."

It was too late! Waves of energy blasted from the weapon, knocking Superman to the dusty ground. Gritting his teeth, Superman tried to push against the tremendous force.

"Can't . . . move!" gasped the Man of Steel. "Feels like . . . I'm getting heavier!"

"That's because you *are*, Superman," Terra-Man said. "My alien step-pa made me all kinds of weapons. This one here makes an *hombre* super-heavy."

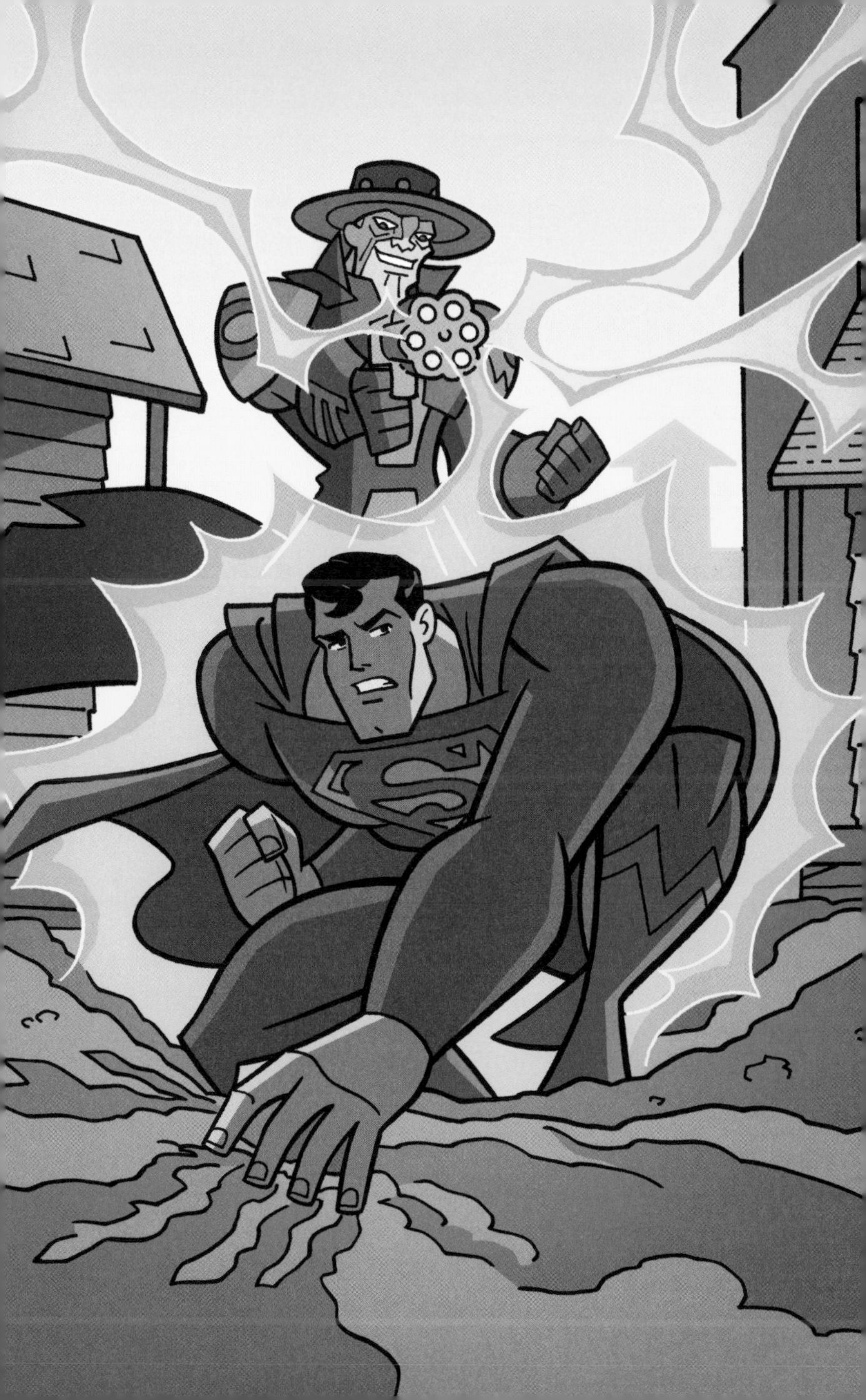

Superman was being crushed under his own weight. Even with his super-strength, he was unable to lift an arm. He could barely breathe. It was like nothing he had ever felt before.

"You're a thousand times heavier than normal, partner," said Terra-Man with a smile. "A normal man would've been crushed to death by now."

The Man of Steel felt himself begin to sink. Then, the ground beneath the super-heavy Superman gave way.

Superman plunged through the solid ground like a pebble sinking in a lake.

"*Hasta luego, amigo*," Terra-Man said. "That means 'see you later, friend!'"

# CHAPTER 4

# TUMBLING TUMBLEWEEDS

Terra-Man chuckled. He spun his energy blaster on his finger and then slipped the weapon back into its holster.

The outlaw patted Nova on the horse's powerful neck. "Guess Superman ain't as tough as we heard," the outlaw bragged. "I was hoping he'd put up a better fight."

Terra-Man hopped off of Nova's back. "Oh, well," he continued. "I guess we don't have to worry about him bothering us from now on."

Then the space outlaw started walking. He passed through an alleyway between an old dress shop and a saloon. Nova followed behind him obediently.

"We got a lot of ground to cover before we can hightail it back home," Terra-Man said. "Now let's get searchin'. Keep your eyes open, Nova."

The white horse shook his head up and down as if to say 'yes.' Then, Nova lowered his head and sniffed. The horse carefully searched the ground in front of him just like Terra-Man was doing.

"It's got to be around here somewhere," Terra-Man muttered. "We'll check every inch of this town until we find it!"

Nova stopped suddenly and reared back on his hind legs in surprise.

Terra-Man looked around but saw no threat. He was puzzled.

"What's wrong, Nova?" the outlaw said. He drew his energy blasters. His eyes darted back and forth, looking for danger. "I don't see anything, boy!"

With an explosive roar, the ground at Terra-Man's feet burst into a blinding cloud of dirt. **SMASH!** The outlaw fell backward. He threw his arms up to protect his eyes from the dust.

"No!" said Superman, who erupted from the ground like he had been shot from a cannon. "*Now* you don't see anything!"

Nova charged through the blinding storm of dust. But Superman saw him coming. The Man of Steel grabbed one of the reins and leaped onto Nova's saddle.

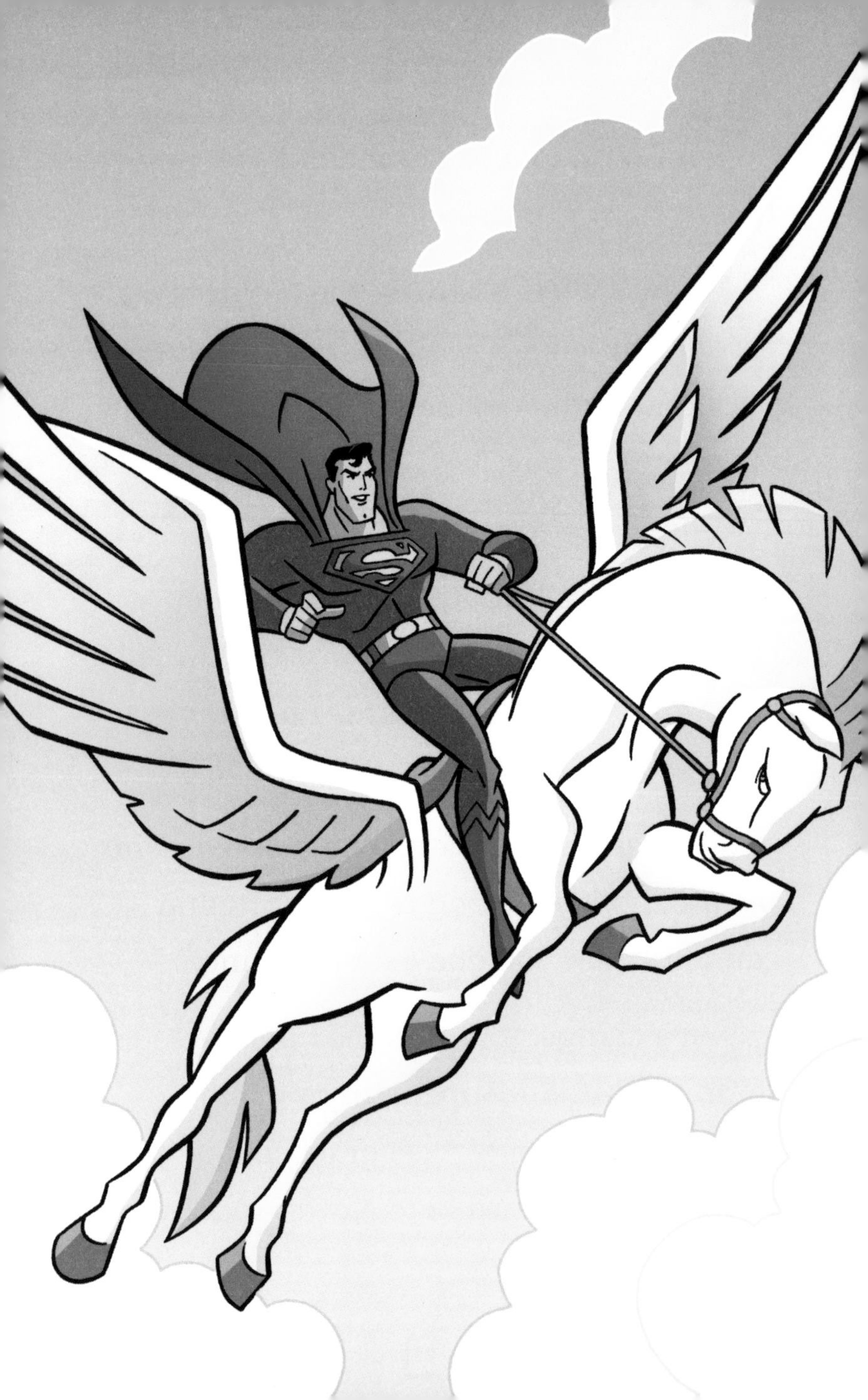

Nova bucked wildly in protest. The horse began to kick and thrash in the air. Superman held on tightly, clinging to the stallion like a rodeo rider.

"Easy, Nova!" Superman said. "I'm not going to hurt you."

"Well isn't that sweet of you," snarled Terra-Man.

The outlaw wiped dust from his eyes with the back of his hand. With the other, he quickly reached for something inside his cowboy hat.

"Too bad we're not going to be so nice in return," he said to Superman.

Suddenly, Terra-Man threw what looked like a handful of twigs into the air. The twigs grew into giant, eight-foot-tall tumbleweeds.

"Now, Nova!" Terra-Man yelled.

The horse lurched violently. Surprised, Superman lost his grip on the reins. He flew through the air. Suddenly, the tumbleweeds rushed at him like bees to honey.

Superman saw them coming. Before he could fly out of their path, something wrapped around his leg. It was Terra-Man's lasso! The outlaw's powerful rope held the Man of Steel down. Soon, the tumbleweeds caught Superman. They wrapped around his body.

The giant plants moved their branches like snakes. For every weed Superman swatted away, three others raced at him. Before he knew it, he was trapped inside the grip of the terrible tumbleweeds.

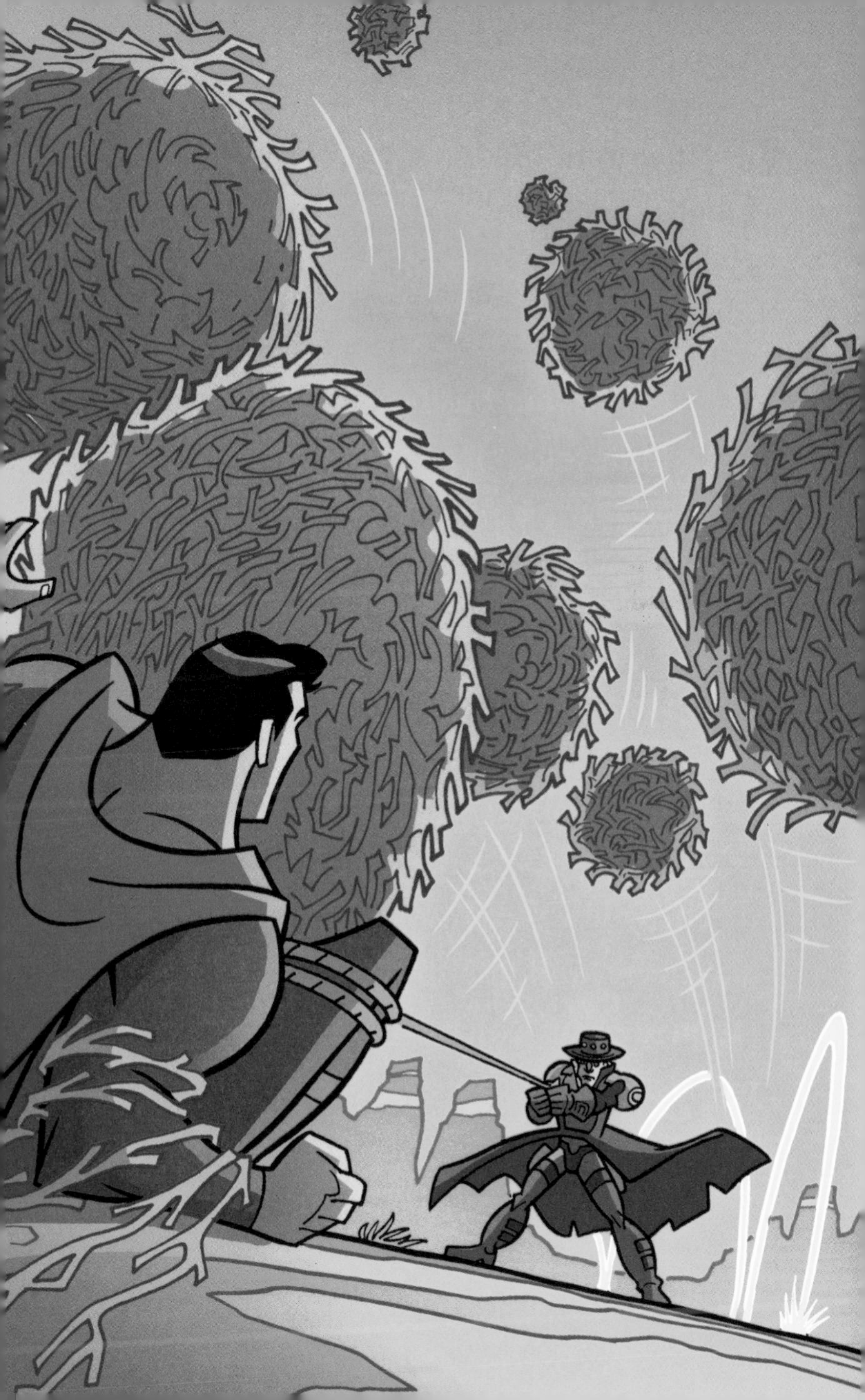

Superman tried to break through the tangled twigs, but the thin branches refused to snap. They stretched like rubber bands in his iron grip.

"Forget about bustin' out, Superman," Terra-Man said. "These are unbreakable alien weeds. Try not to get caught in the wind, partner!"

The cluster of twigs trapping Superman began to roll across the ground. He was caught inside a giant tumbleweed!

**WHOOOOSH!**

The wild weeds lifted him along up, up and away, and into the sky. Terra-Man laughed as he watched the Man of Steel tumble away.

# CHAPTER 5

# SHOWDOWN AT CRIPPLE CREEK

Superman waited until Terra-Man could no longer see him. He took a deep breath, and blew super-cold air on the tangled tumbleweeds. In seconds, his breath froze the twigs solid, making them as brittle as glass. He flexed his muscles, and the frozen plants shattered. He was free from the terrible twigs.

Superman didn't return to Cripple Creek to face off against Terra-Man. Instead, he sped back to the hills where the alien lawmen were waiting.

"I think I found out why Terra-Man is here," Superman told the alien lawmen. "And I've found a way to stop him."

"Tell us, Superman," Tyrox asked eagerly. "His weapons have always been too powerful for us."

"If this plan works, then his weapons won't be a problem," Superman said. He reached into a pouch in his cape and removed a small, yellow orb. It was the size of a golf ball.

"I found this when Terra-Man made me sink into the earth," said Superman.

• • •

The terrible heat at high noon did not stop Terra-Man and Nova from their search. They walked up and down every street and alley.

Terra-Man paced back and forth over every inch of Cripple Creek. He checked each building, one by one.

For the first time in a century, the outlaw from space was sweating. He pulled a bandana from his back pocket and wiped his forehead.

"I don't get it, Nova," Terra-Man said. "Step-pa's notes said this was where he left it! So why isn't it here?"

"Maybe because someone else found it first," said Superman. He stepped out from the doorway of an old saloon.

Superman held out his hand. "Is this what you're looking for, Terra-Man?" In his palm, he held the glowing orb.

"The power pack!" cried Terra-Man in surprise.

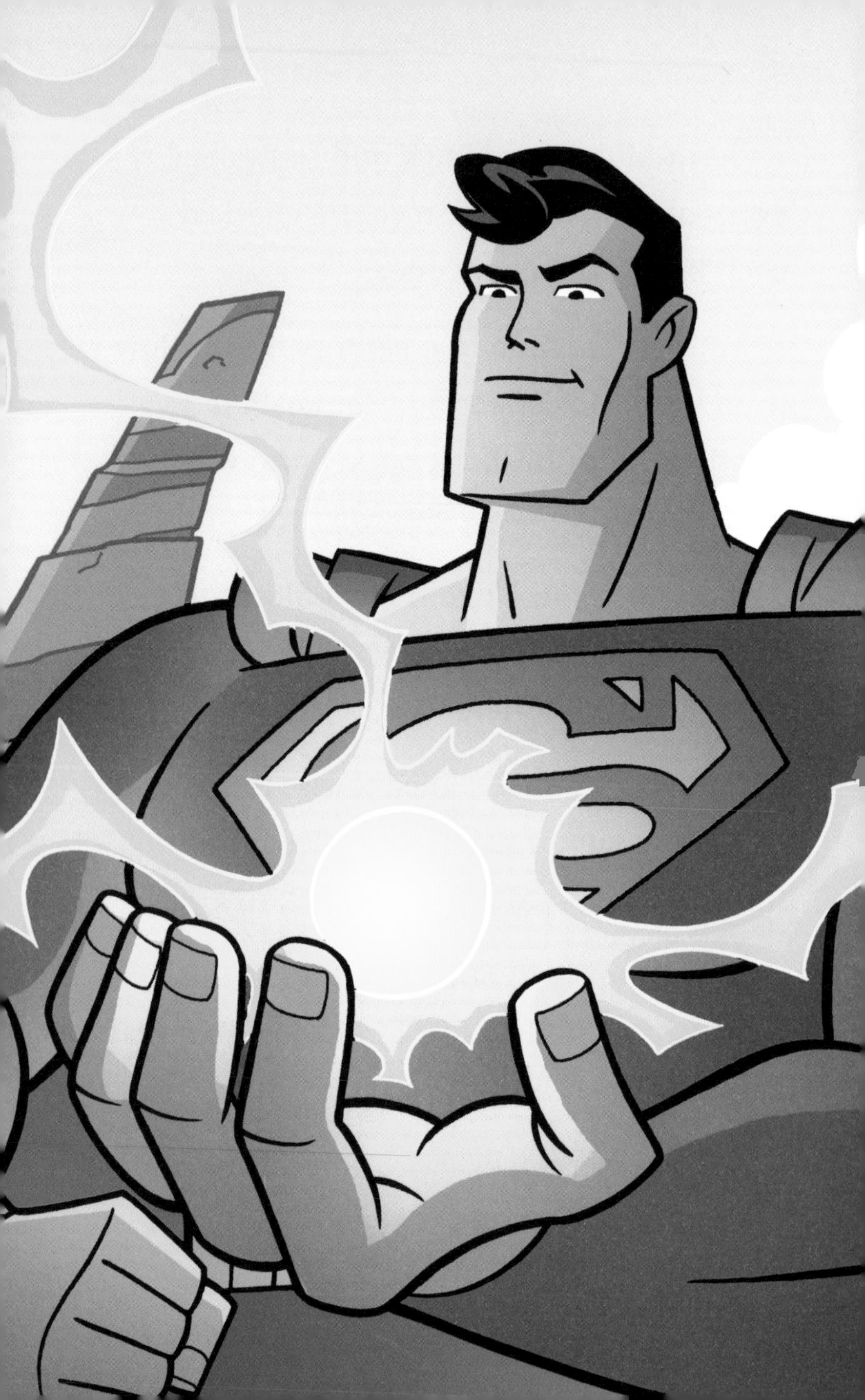

Terra-Man whipped out his blasters and aimed them at Superman. The Man of Steel strolled out to the middle of the street.

"It was buried under Main Street," Superman said. "I wouldn't have found it if you hadn't made me sink into the ground."

"I came halfway across the galaxy for that little gadget!" Terra-Man growled. "So you better hand it over. Pronto!"

Superman closed his fist around the glowing orb.

"It's mine now, Terra-Man," said Superman. "I'm betting that none of your weapons or powers will work without it."

"You got it half-right," said Terra-Man. "The power pack has all the energy needed to power me and Nova for more than one hundred years."

"My alien step-pa hid power packs all over the universe, in case of an emergency," Terra-Man said. "That's why he was on Earth so long ago — to hide that one."

"But you got the other half wrong," the outlaw continued. "I don't gotta be holding the power pack to use its energy. I just gotta be close to it. And this is more than close enough, partner!"

Terra-Man readied his energy blasters. He laughed as he pulled the triggers of the weapons.

Nothing happened. The outlaw stopped laughing. The once powerful weapons were now useless.

"Something's wrong," Terra-Man shouted. "Get him, Nova!"

The winged mustang snorted in anger as he tried to take flight. The great horse's wings flapped, but he could not leave the ground. Like Terra-Man's blasters, Nova's powers no longer worked.

"What in tarnation is going on?!" said the angry outlaw.

Superman grinned. "You made a mistake coming to my planet to start trouble, space cowboy," he said.

"We'll see about that!" Terra-Man said. He shoved his blasters back into their holsters. "I don't need shootin' irons for the likes of you!"

Terra-Man quickly uncoiled an energy whip from his side. He moved toward Superman, smiling. Then he raised his arm, ready to whip the Man of Steel.

Terra-Man snapped the energy whip several times in the air. Its deadly tip made a sharp **SNAP!** in the still air.

"Be careful with that thing," Superman warned. "You could hurt somebody."

"That's just what I intend!" Terra-Man snarled. He stepped toward Superman, the whip snapping closer and closer to the Man of Steel. **SNAP! SNAP!**

Superman's hand reached out at super-speed and grabbed the whip. Terra-Man gasped in surprise. Then, with a flick of his wrist, the Man of Steel jerked the whip from the outlaw's hand.

Terra-Man took a step back. "Ain't no one ever done that before," he said.

"That's because no one knew about your power pack before," said Superman.

Superman made the shape of a gun with his hand. Then, he pointed it at Terra-Man.

"Bang!" said the Man of Steel.

Then, with his super-breath, he blew a blast of air at the outlaw. Terra-Man landed hard on his back.

"Ooof!" grunted Terra-Man. "Hey! This isn't fair!"

*WHOOOOSH!* Superman kept blowing. Terra-Man rolled across the ground, just like the tumbleweeds that had trapped Superman.

Terra-Man rolled helplessly across the desert. Then he came to a sudden stop inside a glowing energy-cage. He was trapped within its powerful bars. In another cage near Terra-Man sat his stubborn stallion, Nova.

Balther, Tyrox, Charop, Kharr, and Gyyhwn came out from the rocks where they had been hiding. In their hands, Balther and Kharr each held a device. They were controlling the energy-cages that imprisoned Terra-Man and Nova.

"Let me outta here, you dirty snakes!" shouted the outlaw. Nova whinnied angrily at the lawmen.

Terra-Man grabbed the glowing bars of his energy-cage. "I'm Terra-Man, dagnabbit!" he said. "There's never been a prison that could hold me!"

"That was before your weapons ran out of power," said Superman. "My police officer friends here surrounded your power source with a special force field. That's what's blocking the power pack's energy from reaching you and Nova."

"Thank you, Superman," said Charop.

Balther stepped forward and stuck out his hand sideways and upside-down toward Superman. "This is how you earthlings say thanks, right?" Balther asked.

The Man of Steel smiled. He shook the lawman's hand. "Close enough," he said, holding in a laugh.

"We never could have apprehended Terra-Man without your help," Kharr said. "It has been a pleasure working with you, Superman."

Balther added, "We'll make sure that Terra-Man never bothers you, or this planet, ever again."

"Always glad to help put an owlhoot like this *hombre* in the hoosegow, partners!" Superman said with a broad smile.

For a moment, the Man of Steel felt just like a sheriff in one of the old Western shows he had watched as a boy.

"Owlhoot? Partners?" questioned Gyyhwn. "I do not understand what these words mean."

"And what is a hoosegow?" asked Balther.

"Well, my friends," said Superman with a smile. "The hoosegow is where Terra-Man's going to be for a very, *very* long time!"

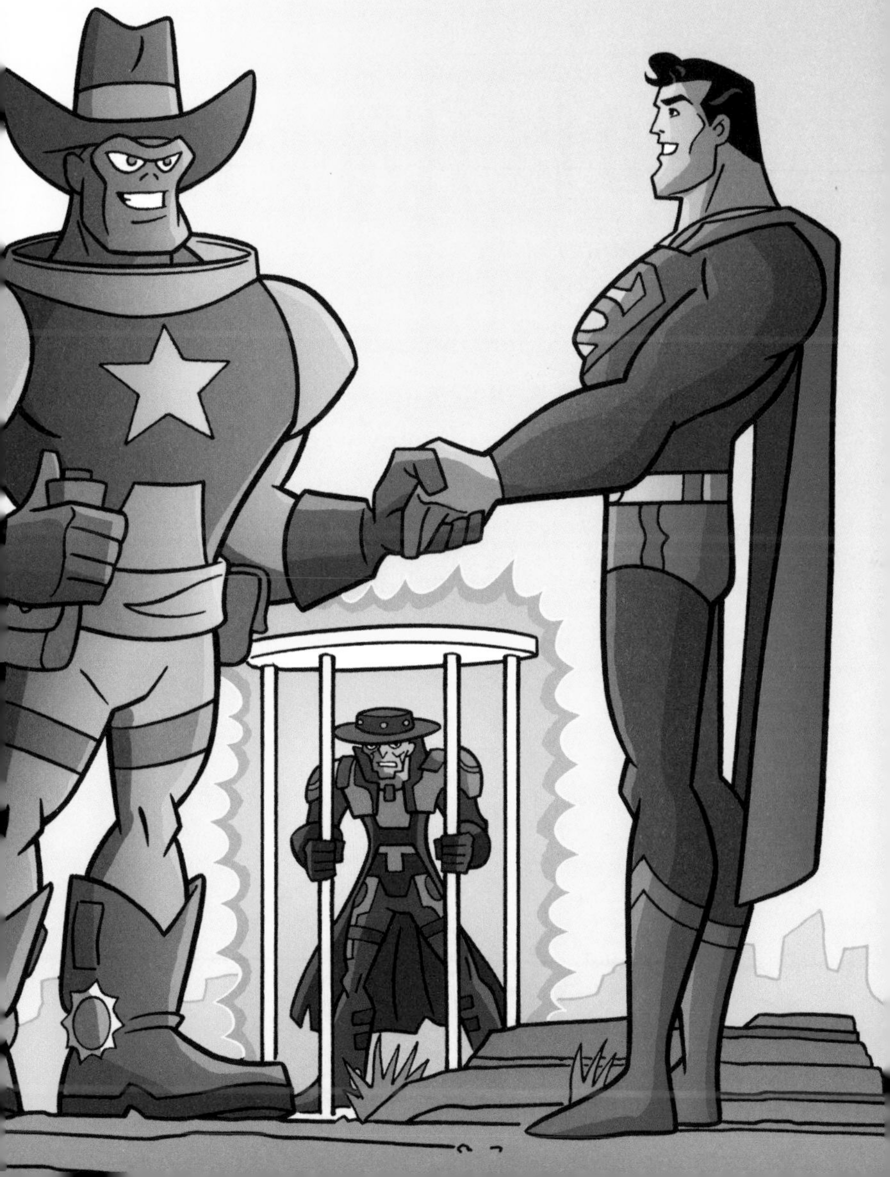

## DAILY PLANET

# WHO IS TERRA-MAN?

Toby Manning's father was an Old West outlaw who was training Toby to follow in his footsteps. One day, a space alien named the Collector kidnapped the young boy. The Collector raised Toby as his son. He trained the boy to use energy weapons by fashioning them in the style of an Old West outlaw. When Toby grew up, he escaped for Earth upon his white mustang, Nova. He gave himself the name Terra-Man and began his quest to become the greatest outlaw the universe has ever known.

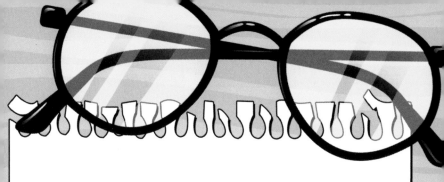

- The Collector's technology granted Terra-Man long life. He appears to be no older than a normal adult male, but he has lived for more than a century!

- Terra-Man's six-shooters are actually high-powered energy blasters capable of stunning even the Man of Steel himself. He also uses entangling tumbleweeds and an energy-lasso to ensnare his enemies.

- The life of a interstellar cowboy involves a lot of space travel. To get him from one solar system to another, Terra-Man rides his white mustang, Nova, at nearly the speed of light! The horse obeys Terra-Man's every command.

- Terra-Man has stolen many different kinds of technology. He even managed to get his hands on a time-traveling device, which he used to steal technology from the future.

# BIOGRAPHIES

**Paul Kupperberg** has written many books for kids, like *Powerpuff Girls: Buttercup's Terrible Temper Tantrums* and *Hey, Sophie!* He has also written more than 600 comic stories involving Superman, the Justice League, Spider-Man, Scooby Doo, and many others. Paul's own character creations include Arion: Lord of Atlantis, Checkmate, and Takion. He has also been an editor for DC Comics and World Wrestling Entertainment. Paul lives in Connecticut with his wife Robin, son Max, and dog, Spike.

**Erik Doescher** is a freelance illustrator and video game designer from Dallas, Texas. Erik illustrated for a number of comic studios in the 1990s, and then moved to Texas to pursue video game development and design. However, he still illustrates his favorite comic book characters.

**Mike DeCarlo** is a longtime contributor of comic art ranging from Batman to Scooby-Doo. He lives in Connecticut with his wife and their four children.

**Lee Loughridge** has been working in comics for more than 14 years. He currently lives in sunny California in a tent on the beach.

# GLOSSARY

**apprehended** (ap-ree-HEND-id)—captured and arrested someone

**cautious** (KAW-shuhss)—if you are cautious, you try to avoid mistakes and danger

**harsh** (HARSH)—unpleasant or rough

*hombre* (OM-bray)—a Spanish word meaning "guy" or "fellow"

**obedient** (oh-BEE-dee-uhnt)—if you are obedient, you do what you are told to do

**reins** (RAYNZ)—straps attached to a horse's neck that are used to guide the horse

**saloon** (suh-LOON)—a bar from the Old West where people could drink and eat

**shattered** (SHAT-urd)—broke into tiny pieces

**villain** (VIL-uhn)—a wicked or evil person

# DISCUSSION QUESTIONS

1. Superman is famous across the universe for being a super hero. If you could be famous for one thing, what would you choose? Why?

2. Who has cooler superpowers — Superman or Terra-Man? Explain your answer.

3. Clark Kent is secretly Superman. Why do you think he keeps his identity a secret? If you were a super hero, would you tell anyone?

# WRITING PROMPTS

1. Terra-Man travels the universe on Nova, his white mustang. If you could have your own animal to ride, what would it be? Write a description, and then draw a picture of it.

2. Pretend that you're an alien who has just seen Earth for the very first time. Describe our planet from an alien's perspective. What do humans do that might seem strange to a visitor from space?

3. Imagine that Terra-Man manages to escape from prison. Write a story where Terra-Man battles with the Man of Steel one last time.

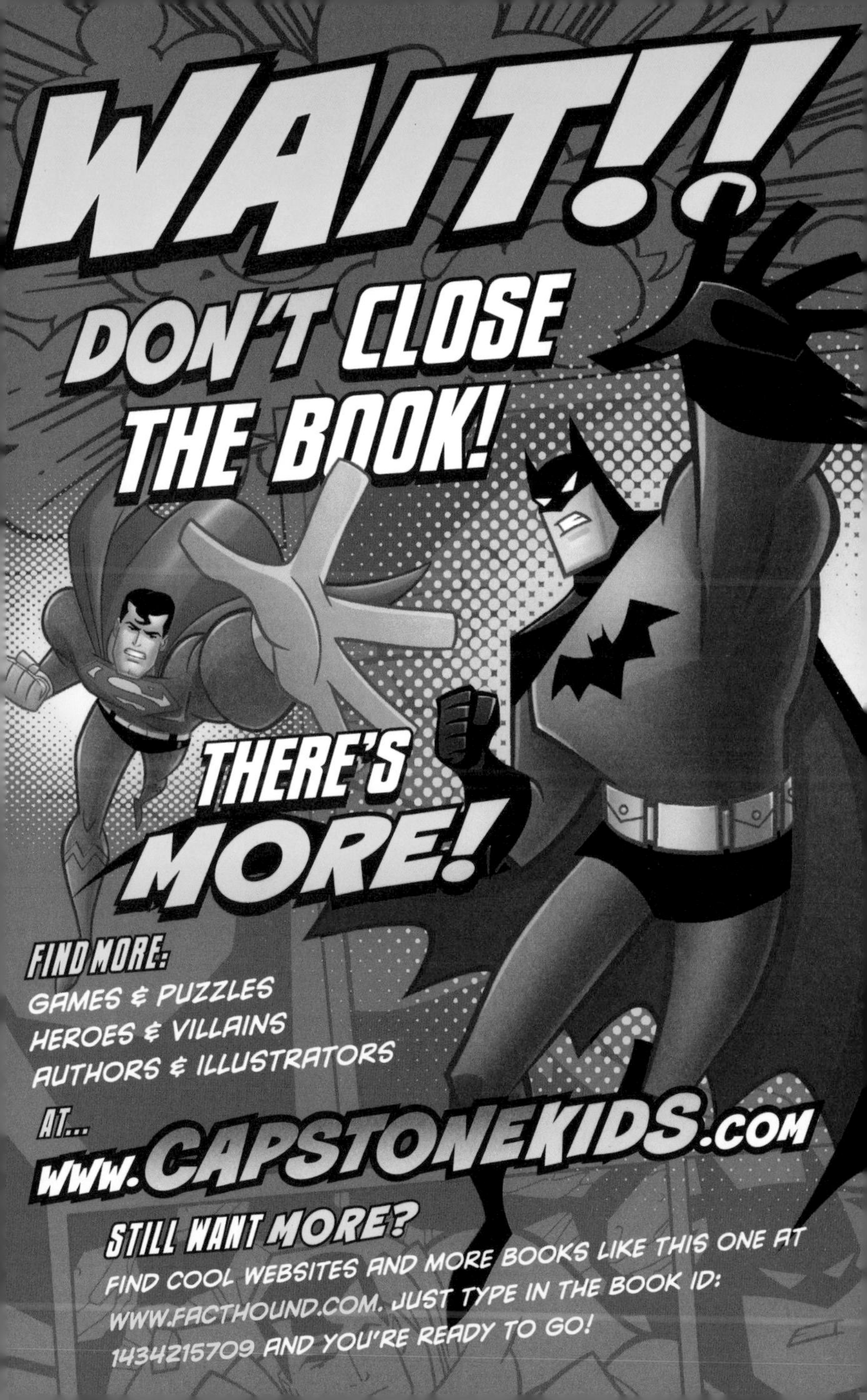
WAIT!!
DON'T CLOSE THE BOOK!
THERE'S MORE!
FIND MORE:
GAMES & PUZZLES
HEROES & VILLAINS
AUTHORS & ILLUSTRATORS
AT...
WWW.CAPSTONEKIDS.COM
STILL WANT MORE?
FIND COOL WEBSITES AND MORE BOOKS LIKE THIS ONE AT
WWW.FACTHOUND.COM. JUST TYPE IN THE BOOK ID:
1434215709 AND YOU'RE READY TO GO!

# MORE NEW SUPERMAN ADVENTURES!

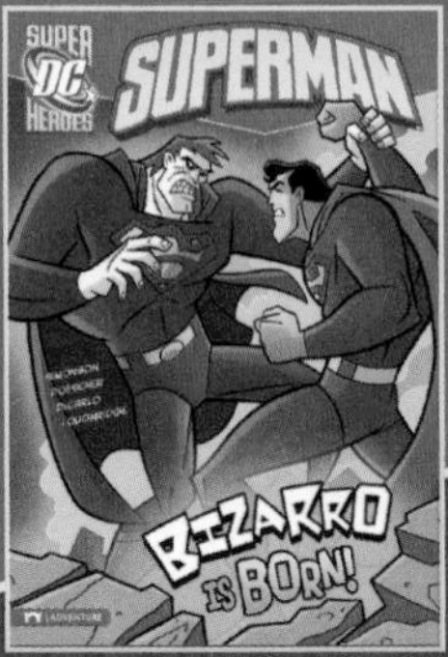
SUPER DC HEROES
SUPERMAN
BIZARRO IS BORN!

BIZARRO IS BORN!

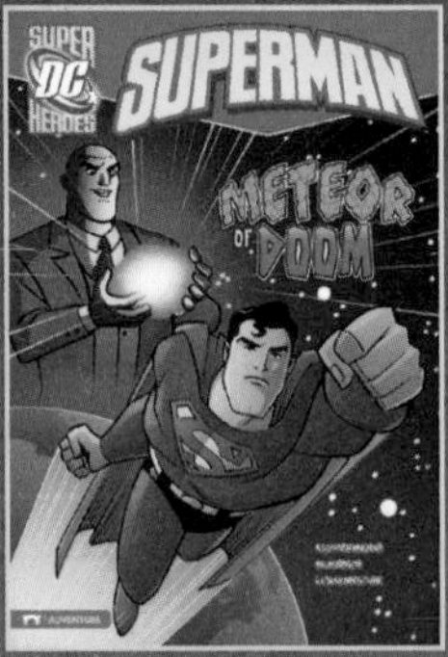
SUPER DC HEROES
SUPERMAN
METEOR OF DOOM

METEOR OF DOOM

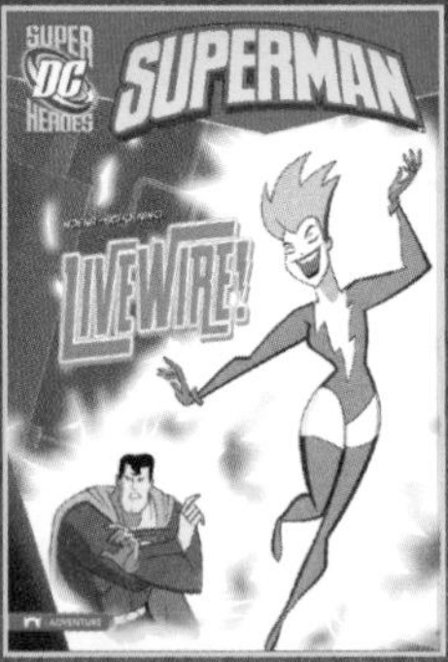
SUPER DC HEROES
SUPERMAN
LIVEWIRE!

LIVEWIRE!

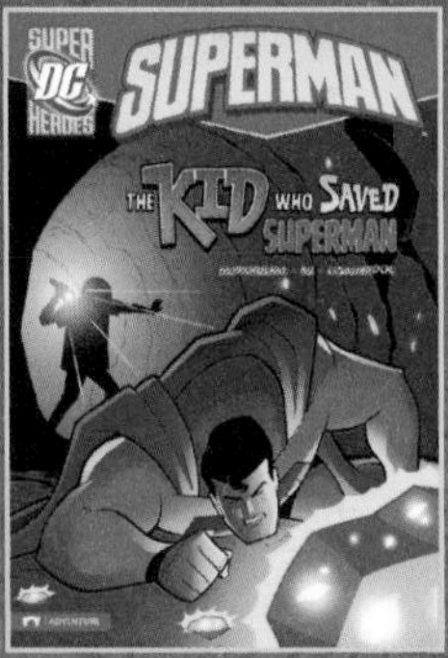
SUPER DC HEROES
SUPERMAN
THE KID WHO SAVED SUPERMAN

THE KID WHO SAVED SUPERMAN

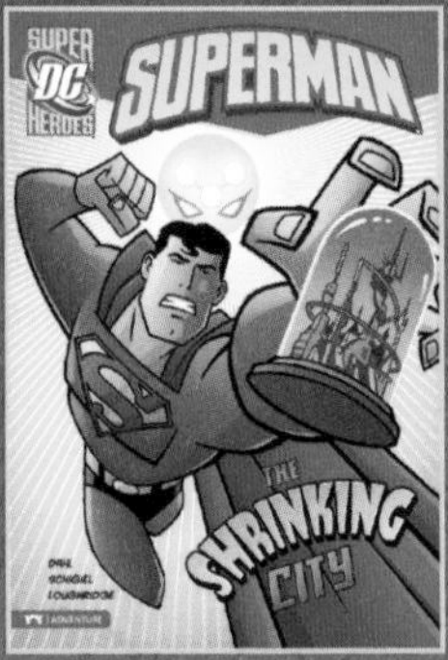
SUPER DC HEROES
SUPERMAN
THE SHRINKING CITY

THE SHRINKING CITY

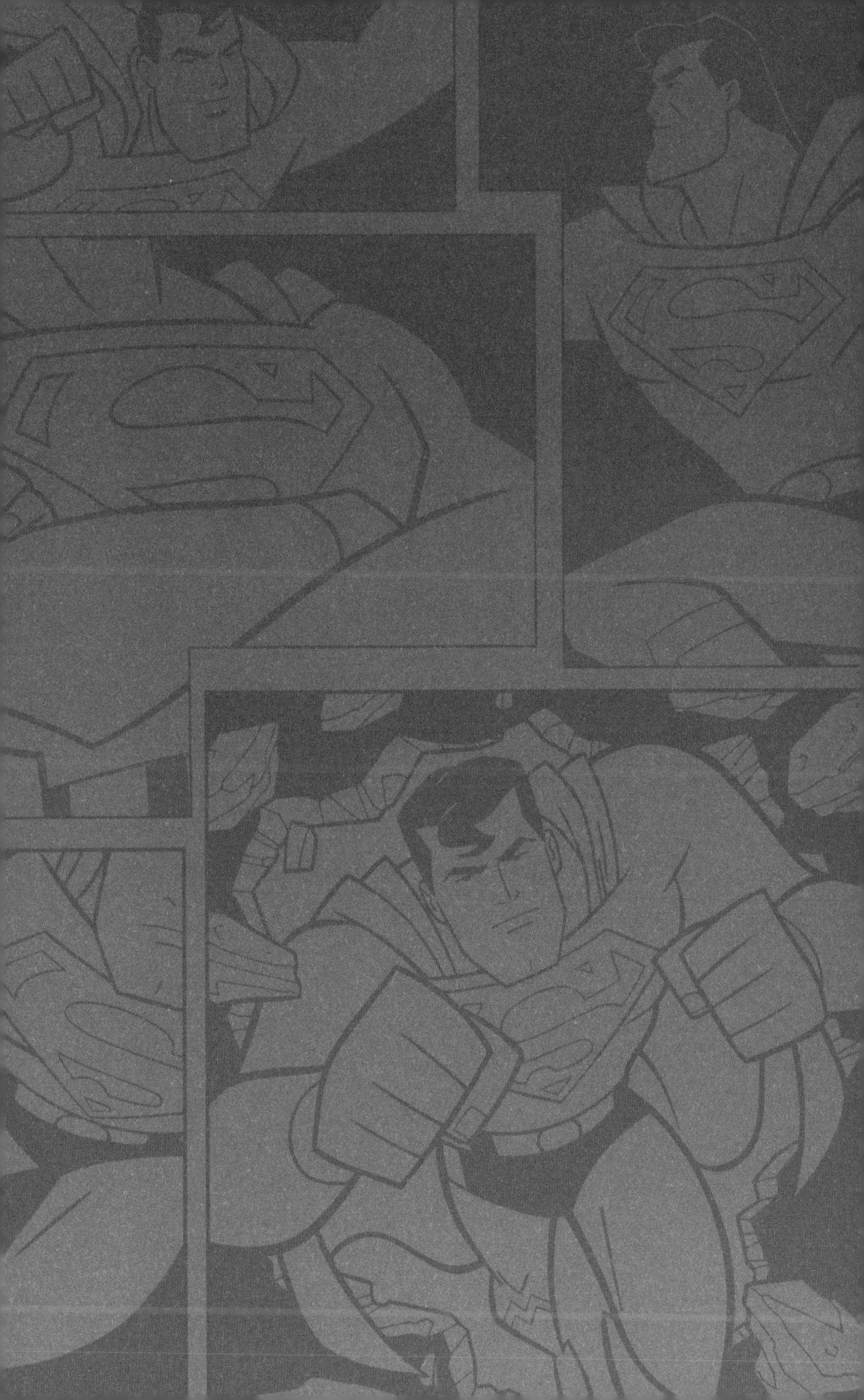

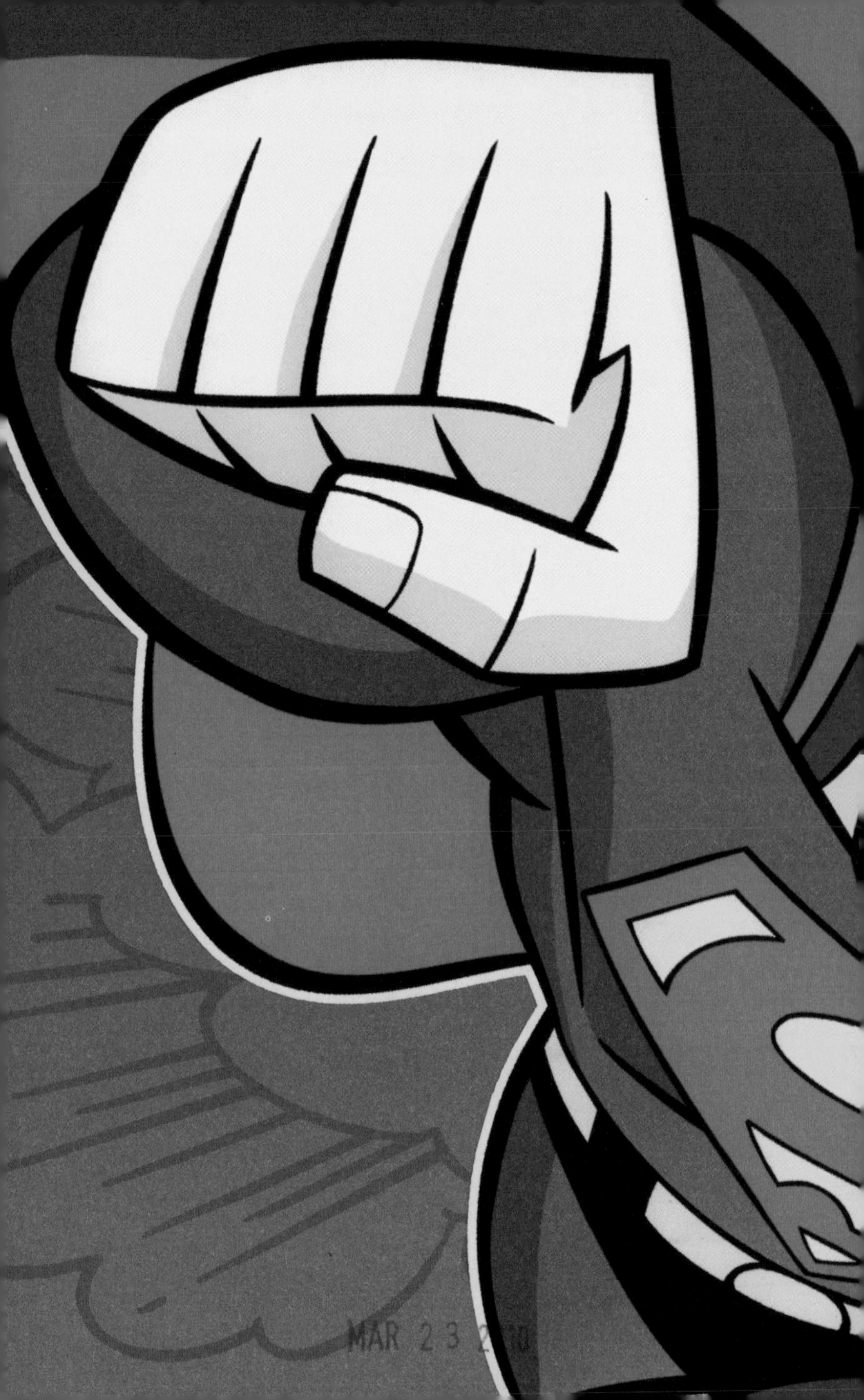